Guess What I Found in DRAGON WOOD

Timothy Knapman

illustrated by Gwen Millward

Guess What I Found in DRAGON WOOD

BLOOMSBURY
CHILDREN'S
BOOKS

You'll never **guess** what I found the other day.

It's called a Benjamin. I didn't know what to
do with it, so I took it home to show my parents.

Mom thought it might want to eat something, so she cooked it a delicious meal with all the **stinkiest** fish and the **slimiest, yuckiest worms.** But it turned out it wasn't hungry.

"Can the Benjamin sleep in my room tonight, Mom?" I asked.

"I don't know if it's ever slept in a bed before," said Mom, "but it does look very tired."

So I gave it some pajamas. **And guess what!** Its feet weren't striped after all!

↑
These are called "rain boots."

The next morning, I took it to meet my friends.

"We're going to school," I said. "Today, we're going to learn how to sit on a volcano!"

The Benjamin didn't look very happy.

Marvin

Maybe they don't have any schools where it comes from.

Gus

Henry

~The~
DRAGONWOOD
ACADEMY

Mr. Crockface

The second he saw the Benjamin, Mr. Crockface
said Volcano Sitting class was canceled.

After all, you don't get to meet a Benjamin
every day of the week—and we were sure to
learn a lot from something so strange.

And the Benjamin was **very** strange!

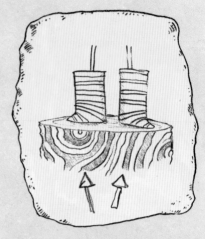

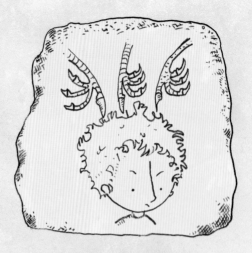

It could get around
without wings.

It had soft, fluffy
stuff on its head.

Where had all its
scales gone?

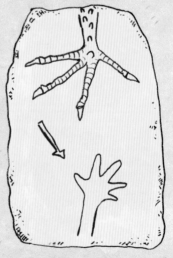

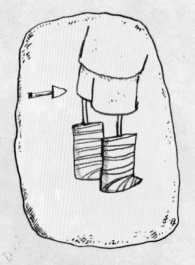

Its claws weren't
sharp at all!

Its tail had
fallen off.

No wonder its roar was
more like a squeak!

This is called a tear.
It's a sad thing.

And instead of breathing fire from its nostrils,
it leaked water from its eyes!

That's how we found out that the Benjamin was homesick. So he told us all about the faraway, magical land he came from . . . a land **full** of Benjamins!

Daddy Benjamins ↑

Boy Benjamins ↑ ↑

Girl Benjamins ↑

and Mommy Benjamins ↑

Can you believe it?

They think dragons are make-believe and are found only in books!

"So," I said, "you don't fly, you don't roar, you don't breathe fire— **what DO you do?**"

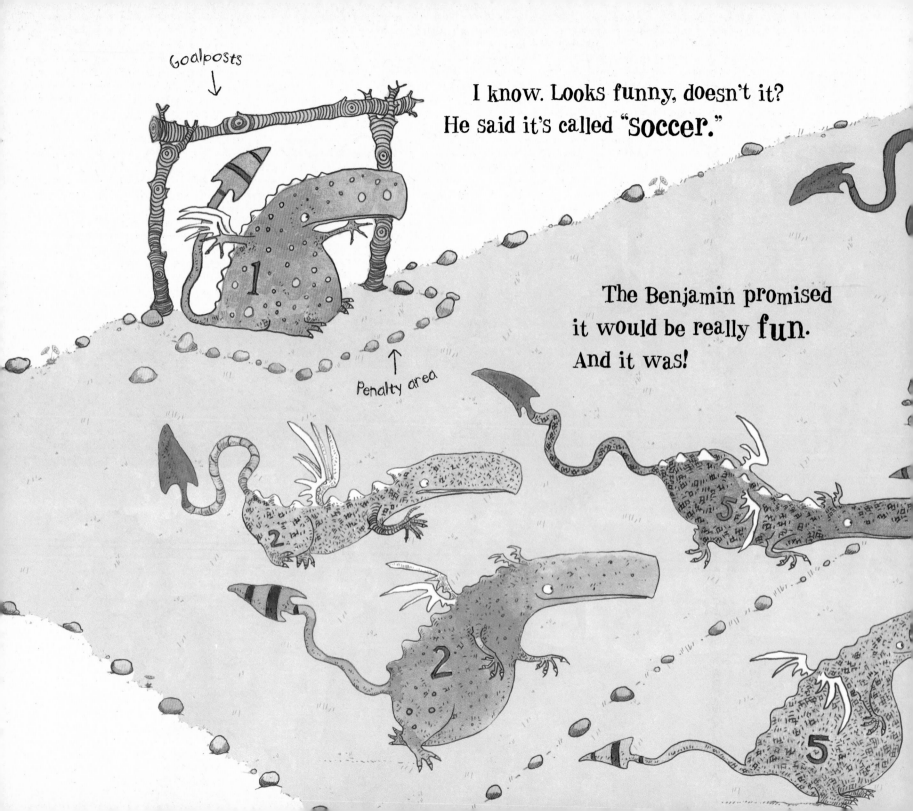

Referee

Ball

My team colors

You're not supposed to fly in the penalty area though. Or eat the ball. OR burn down the goalposts. There are so many things to remember!

We had such a fun afternoon, but when I said it was time to go home, the Benjamin looked like he was going to leak again.

"You miss your mom and dad, don't you?" I asked, and the Benjamin nodded yes. "I'll miss **you**," I said, but I knew it was time for him to go. "Don't worry, I'll take you home."

You see, I really wanted to take a look at the land of the Benjamins. I asked my friends if they'd like to come with us, but I think they were all **too scared**.

I was a bit **anxious** myself. I only knew one Benjamin, so I didn't know what a whole country **full** of them would be like.

But the Benjamin was getting so excited about going home, I couldn't help smiling.

Woo-hoo!

far, far across the seas . . .

It was an awfully long way.

But it was just
as beautiful as
he said it would be.

I have to tell you
something though. The
Benjamins sure do
have a funny way of
saying hello.

When I got back home, I told all my friends about everything!
I told them about the wheely boxes with **wee-woo** noises
and the **whip-whip-whirly-birds** with spotlights.
They were very excited.

"Do you ever want to go back again?" they asked.

"Of course," I said. "The Benjamin wants
to take me to school to meet his teacher."

Or was that **EAT** his teacher?

I wasn't **quite** sure.

I've got to go now...

Soccer practice!

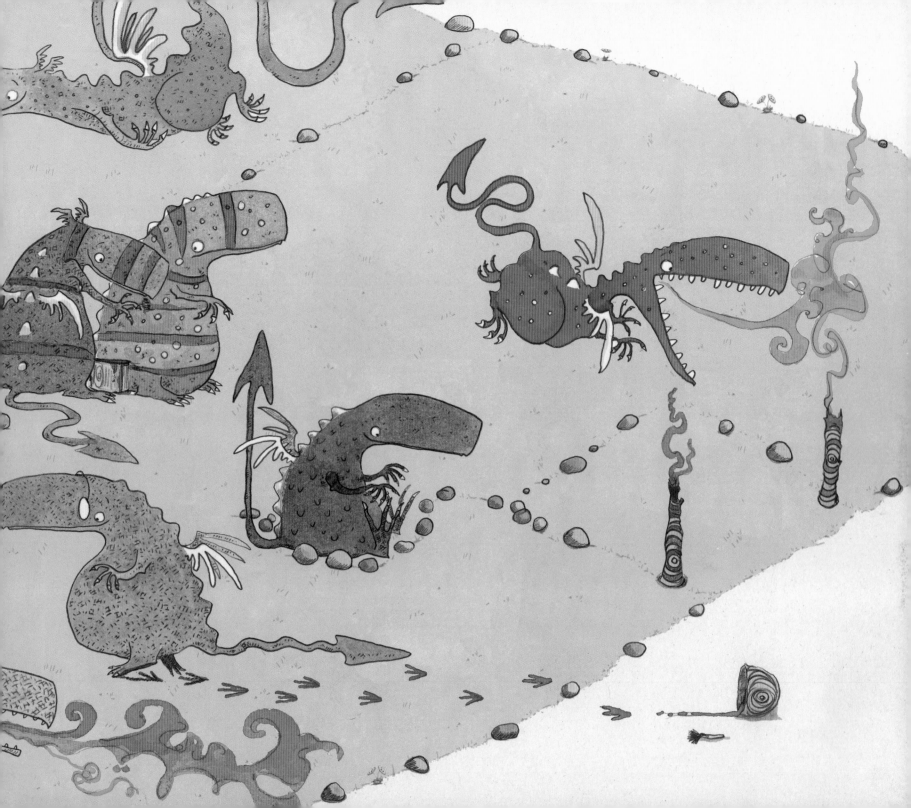

For all my faraway readers, especially
Addison, Tucker, Spencer, Keir, and Maddy, with love —T. K.

For Will —G. M.

Text copyright © 2007 by Timothy Knapman • Illustrations copyright © 2007 by Gwen Millward
First published in Great Britain in 2007 by Puffin Books Ltd UK

Typeset in Blue Century
Art created with watercolor and pencil

Published by Bloomsbury U.S.A. Children's Books, 175 Fifth Avenue, New York, NY 10010
Distributed to the trade by Holtzbrinck Publishers

Library of Congress Cataloging-in-Publication Data available upon request
ISBN-13: 978-1-59990-190-9 • ISBN-10: 1-59990-190-0

First U.S. Edition 2008
Printed in China
1 3 5 7 9 10 8 6 4 2